# THE STORY KEEPERS

Episode 5

# Sink or Swim

Brian Brown and Andrew Melrose

CASSELL

**Cassell**
Wellington House, 125 Strand,
London WC2R 0BB

© Brian Brown and
Andrew Melrose, 1997

First published 1997

**British Library Cataloguing-
in-Publication Data**
A catalogue record for this
book is available from the
British Library.

ISBN 0-304-33679-3

Long ago, in the city of Rome,
there lived a mighty ruler.
His name was Nero.
He thought he was a god,
but the Christians knew he wasn't.
So Nero hated them.

One day there was a great fire.
Nero said the Christians started it,
and he sent his cruel soldiers after them.

Marcus, Justin, and Anna
lost their parents during the fire.
Ben the baker and his wife, Helena,
took them into their home.
There, in a time of great danger,
they told the children stories about Jesus.

This book is about the adventures
of the Storykeepers.

It was a dark, stormy night in
the city of Rome.
In the bakery Cyrus and Anna
were juggling rolls.
"I can't do six," said Anna.
"Yes, you can!" Cyrus replied. "Here!"
He tossed her six rolls hot from the oven.
"Ow!" Anna said, juggling faster and faster.
"I knew you could do it!" Cyrus laughed.

A knock sounded at the door. "Who can that be?" said Helena. Ben opened the door. A man lay on the doorstep.
"Ben," the man groaned.
"Titus!" said Ben. He picked up the man and carried him to bed.

Later, Titus told them what had happened.
"Because I am a Christian, the Roman soldiers sent me to a slave ship," he said. "It was terrible. The captain was cruel, and we hardly had any food. I escaped when we came ashore."

"My father was on a slave ship, too.
Do you know him?" asked Justin.
"There are many ships and hundreds
of slaves," Titus replied.
"How can we help them, Ben?"
asked Justin.
"We'll take our show to the ship!"
answered Ben.

The next day, Ben and the
gang set up their show on
the deck. The soldiers
and sailors watched Anna and
Cyrus juggle.
Justin and Ben hid in the lower
part of the ship. Zak passed food
to them through a porthole.

Justin took loaves to the slaves down below. "What are you doing here, boy?" a slave named Andrew asked. "I'm looking for my father," Justin replied.

"The only thing you'll find here is trouble," Andrew said. "Now go, before you get us all killed."

Suddenly a guard shouted: "All slaves to the oars! The captain has ordered us to sea."
Ben, Helena, Zak, and the children scrambled to leave the ship.
Too late! They were trapped on board, far from shore.

A sailor led them to the captain's
cabin. He locked the door.
The ship began to roll. The children
were frightened. They had never
been to sea before.
So Ben told them a story Jesus told.

The rains fell.
The floods came.
The winds blew.
The houses rocked, just as this
ship is doing right now.
The house built on the rock
stood firm.
But the other house came down
with a crash.

Suddenly the door burst open.
Hadrian the Fearless, the captain, stood in
the doorway.
"So these are the stowaways!" said Hadrian.
"They will work like everyone else."

"Take this mop," the captain said to Zak.

"You, give water to the soldiers," he ordered Justin.

"And you two stay here and clean," he said to Marcus and Cyrus.

"I'm a baker," said Ben.

"Excellent!" Hadrian said. "Go to the galley at once!"

The mate took Ben, Helena, and Anna to the kitchen.

The cook was preparing soup for the slaves. It looked awful.

"I'm supposed to help with the bread," said Ben.

"Good. I could use some help," said the cook.

Soon, the smell of warm baked bread filled the kitchen. "Mmm. What is that?" the cook asked. "Our special bread. Here, taste some," Helena offered. While the cook gobbled the bread, Ben made fresh good soup for the prisoners.

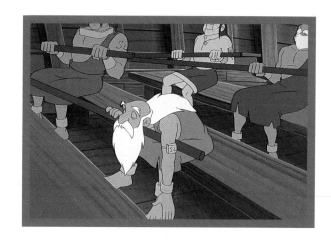

Meanwhile, Justin took water to the guards.
One of the slaves begged him for a sip.
But the guard dragged Justin away.
"He's dying of thirst," said Justin. "I'll
take his place."
The guard laughed. "This I've got
to see! Go ahead, little man!"
he scoffed.
So Justin took the man's
place and began
to row.

19

Ben and Helena took the soup to the slaves.
As they ate Ben told them a story.

One day Jesus was teaching people about God's way. The house was packed.

Four people were carrying a friend who couldn't walk. They could not get in.

The four carried their friend on to the roof. They lowered him through the roof to the feet of Jesus.
When Jesus saw how they trusted him, he said to their friend: "Get up, pick up your mat, and walk."

The man got up and began to walk. Everyone was amazed. "We've never seen anything like this!" they said.

The slaves, too, were amazed. They enjoyed the story nearly as much as the soup.

Suddenly, there was a crash.
"We're under attack!" shouted a slave.
"Prepare to be boarded!"
A ship had smashed into the hull.
Water poured into the hold.
Ben and the gang clambered into the soup pot
and floated in the water.

As the pot passed the ship some
slaves called out: "Help us!
We're drowning!"
The gang clambered back on
board.
"They're still chained," said
Justin.

"I saw some keys in the captain's cabin," said Cyrus. Thastus, Marcus's pet goat, butted the door.
The door burst open, and Cyrus found the keys.

Ben helped Helena, Marcus, and Anna
to escape to another ship. He and Justin
took the keys to the slave hold.
By now many of the slaves were waist
deep in water.

Justin took several deep breaths and dived. Could he unlock the slaves in time?

"Hurry. We can't last much longer," they cried.

Just in time, Justin turned the key and set them free.

One slave, Andrew, was left.

The ship was sinking. Justin and Andrew
were still on board.
When all seemed lost, Justin and Andrew
burst from the water.
Thanks to the bravery of Justin, all the
slaves were rescued. Ben and the gang were
picked up by a rebel ship. And everyone
arrived home, safe and sound.

# THE STORY KEEPERS

There are thirteen exciting books
in The Storykeepers series.

Episodes 10–13
Join Ben and the gang for more
narrow escapes as they fight to keep